Abreea Louise
and the
Spirit in the Attic

BETTY ELLIS

ISBN 978-1-63903-206-8 (paperback)
ISBN 978-1-63903-207-5 (digital)

Christian Faith Publishing, Inc.
832 Park Avenue
Meadville, PA 16335
www.christianfaithpublishing.com

Printed in the United States of America

Chapter 1

It was the beginning of spring with flowers blooming, birds singing, and the endless possibilities that spring break would hold. Little did I know what that thought would cost me. It's as though my thoughts of not wanting to return to school had conjured up this rising nightmare. As luck would have it, and I don't believe in luck, we did not return to school after spring break. This was the stuff of my dreams. Right! A resounding *no*!

It all began when every conversation from every adult was about a deadly virus sweeping China, Italy, and other foreign countries. Yet I felt secure because we are the United States, with the best of everything, and it would not come here. When we left school on Friday for spring break, we had full expectations that we would be returning within a week.

I had that one long glorious week to do exactly what I wanted to do. I loved sleeping late, staying up late, reading, watching old movies, and doing any kind of art. In fact, when I grow up (and I hate that statement when adults say it), I am going to be an artist. I don't know what kind of artist; just an artist. Aunt Sissy, who lives in a small coastal town in Southeast Georgia, is always trying to get my mother to enroll me in art classes, to visit art museums or anything "artsy" that would help me to become an artist, to help me decide what kind of artist I want to be.

I really just wish she would leave me alone. Just because she is a teacher and has taught forever, she thinks she knows what's best about my life. It doesn't help either that Mom thinks she's some kind of know-it-all genesis about teenagers. She's got kids, and they didn't exactly turn out perfect.

Anyway, back to my spring break of doing just what I want to do, and that is nothing. But as usual in my life, fate wouldn't have it that way. The week of spring break started out fine. Then our president said that all schools must close immediately for six weeks. What? This was my dream come true, until reality hit me square in the face. Literally, I had to stay in my house and wear a mask on the few occasions that I might get to go somewhere.

Mom and all the other adults in my family started hoarding toilet paper, anything with sanitizer in it, and flour. How random. Had they all lost their minds? Then the news started showing how people were fighting for these things in the grocery stores. On one occasion, I went to the grocery store with Mom, and I was horrified! The shelves were empty! People passed in the store as though they were scared to death to be in the same room.

My dream of not returning to school had become a nightmare. This is not what I asked for. This is not what I wanted. Then there is the voice of my grandmother on my dad's side pounding in my head. *Be careful what you ask for, little lady. You might just get it and more.* I will never tell her, but I finally realized what she meant all these years. This was truly more than I had asked for.

Because of the pandemic, my mother tried to keep me entertained. There were very few places we could go. So one day, she came up with a bright idea—since my sleeping late was not on her list—that I needed to be busy. It was okay that my older brother, Matt, maintained his social life, working at a pharmacy and meeting his friends at a neighbor's pool. How I detested my brother and all he stood for. He is a ruggedly handsome high school football star. It doesn't help that he has a bunch of friends, not just friends on social media but actual friends who are always at our house. I am not anything like my brother.

On this particular morning, she woke me up and announced that we were going to take a short road trip. I was pleasantly surprised for the first millisecond until I started overthinking, as I always do, just where my scared mother would dare to venture during this pandemic. When I asked if we were going to my aunt's house, she just smiled. I hated that particular smile. I knew she thought it was a fantastic idea, but in the end, I would be miserable. My mom had a knack for such outings, and I was always right, miserable. I was already wishing I could just stay in bed, in my little prison room. At least in there, I didn't have to play the social graces.

As we were driving north, my sickening suspicion was confirmed. We were going to spend the whole long, boring day with Aunt Sissy. I would play their game of smiling and acting interested in their conversation while getting lost on my phone. That is, until I realized I had left my earpieces at home. My day just got worse. I was trapped, with nowhere to go and no way out.

Aunt Sissy lived in a huge house in the woods on a tidal creek near a small South Georgia town. She was not like the rest of my family. She was a little on the artsy side, loved to travel, and loved to talk. She worked in education and seemed to do okay with it. I just got tired of hearing her long answers and advice she would give to parents if they made the mistake of asking her a "What to do with my kid?" type of question. She seemed to always be giving advice to somebody.

My aunt's house was in a gated community that was situated among huge live oak trees. Ducks and Canadian geese frequently visited the two lakes in the neighborhood. You might also see whitetail deer, wild turkeys, and an occasional red-tailed fox. Behind her house was a pier with a dock over a tidal creek. I loved seeing the occasional alligator or dolphins that would swim in search of redfish. It was a unique place to visit. It was like visiting a wild zoo of native animals. There were always wild berries and grapes to eat as you walked through the wooded lots. There were lots of wooded lots since the neighborhood only had seven houses built in it.

So my day was planned. We would arrive, I would be polite, eat my grilled hamburger, which we always had, and then excuse myself to ride her bike. I would spend the day talking to my friends on my phone and taking pictures.

As we pulled into the neighborhood, I was surprised to see two new houses being built by my aunt's house. Well, there's at least some new excitement in this secluded neighborhood where nothing ever seems to change. After excusing myself from lunch, I took a bicycle tour of the community and chatted on the phone.

I decided to get my sketchpad and go to the lakes to draw pictures of the ducks. While I was sitting quietly in my private world, actually enjoying my activity, a voice said, "So you think you can draw?"

I didn't know who had said it, and I didn't care. I jumped up, pencils flying everywhere, to see a boy about my age staring at me face-to-face.

He continued, "Who do you think you are? An artist, or just someone who thinks they are the best at everything?" I let all the rage of living with a brother who fit that bill and being a prisoner in my own head rain on that boy. There was instant hate, and he reciprocated. "Yeah, you're exactly like my friends said all you South Georgia country girls would be."

He just needed to shut up. I didn't like him—the way he looked and the sound of his voice or the way he smelled. "Well, did God just arrive? I don't think so. I picture him as being perfect, something you will never be. I don't know where you are from, and I don't care. And for the record, I am not a South Georgia country bumpkin. I live in White Sand Beach."

"Well, now that just makes everything perfect! You think because you threw around the name of White Sand Beach that I'm going to bow to your highness? Y'all are lame down there. Atlanta is a much better city to live in. We have a major airport, the Atlanta Braves, the Falcons, and loads of fun things to do. Y'all don't have any of that."

"And why would we want it? Your beloved Bulldogs always come to our city to play against our Gators. Plus we have beaches that your nasty butts spoil every summer with your Atlanta litter. So why don't you just stay out of White Sand Beach?"

He totally ruined the only peace I had found at my aunt's house. I quickly gathered my art supplies amid the dreadful sound of his laughter and ran back to Aunt Sissy's.

As I burst into the den, I screamed to my mother, "Can we go now?" And then I realized they were discussing the new neighbors who were building the house next door.

"Breeby." I hated it when my aunt called me Breeby. "Breeby, have you met Cooper?"

"No, and I don't want to meet him! I'm sure he will be just fine, an excellent student who will make loads of friends!"

And there was that look in my mother's eyes. I had overstepped my boundary, so I did what every nice little southern country bumpkin does and apologized.

The story went on that Copper's father was building the house next door. He was an only child of a very bad marriage. So his father thought it was best if he gave Cooper a new start. As bad as I already hated him, I did feel sorry for him. He would be leaving Atlanta to move to Tellico. If that were not punishment enough, he would be moving into a neighborhood with no kids. He would have to change schools, if we ever go to school again, and have to make friends during a pandemic. Yes, I did feel sorry for him, but not sorry enough to offer an apology for my reactions to his insults. I would not tell my mom and aunt of our unfortunate meeting by the lake. I didn't want to be forced to do "the right thing," nor did I want to be told to hang out with the creep. I used the sweltering summer temperature as an excuse not to go back outside.

Because I was young and thin, my aunt sent me on an excursion to the attic to retrieve a piece of furniture she was giving my mom from my grandmother's house. While in the attic, among old things that I could just not believe my aunt had stored was an old cedar chest. It was the kind of chest I had read about in books where young girls kept a chest of things they made for use when they got married. I still struggle with that idea. Why would any sane young teenager want to spend her time crocheting and knitting things for a house and a marriage? Not me. I was going to use these years to enjoy growing up. This was my time, and I was going to take it. I didn't want to turn into my brother, always getting dressed up for a date. I also was not looking forward to turning into my mother.

After delivering the table, I asked my aunt what was in the chest. She took her precious time to tell me all about my grandmother, how she held onto little keepsakes from my grandfather or her children when they were little. Being bored, I figured a venture through the chest might be a distraction from my encounter with Cooper while avoiding having to meet him again. So I asked if I might go through the things in the chest. To my surprise, my aunt who kept everything in its place said yes. Her request was that I did not permanently remove anything and that I put everything back just as I found it.

Little did I know how that one question would change me forever? I often got lost in how people made a simple decision that would have a major impact on a kid's life, such as Cooper's father doing the "right thing" for him. I found that absurd. Surely, he had not asked Cooper how he felt about moving. But then adults never ask their kids anything really important. Their questions are always about homework, social media, or chores. Never had I been asked my opinion on any topic that involved me. If by chance there was that one time, my answer was totally ignored. Why do adults do that? I will not be that kind of parent. Oh no, I am not going to be any kind of parent.

As I started exploring my aunt's attic, I forgot about the time. If it had not been for the attic fan, I would have died of heat exhaustion up there. My mother had handed me some water and told me not to stay up there too long.

I soon found myself entangled with the past. I began wondering about my grandmother. I had always been told that she loved to read and liked to draw but was not very good at completing her artsy projects. With each item discovered, I wondered what my grandmother had used it for, what stories that little night table could have told about my grandmother's life. I wondered if she had fears at night as I do. I wondered why she wanted to marry so young and have so many children. I wondered a lot of things about her that I had never heard my mother or aunt talk about. They talked about everything else; why not about my grandmother?

With the discovery of each new attic treasure, I started reflecting on tidbits of conversations about my grandmother. I realized they had talked of their childhoods and hers; they had often spoken about how she did this or that. Once, my aunt even told me that I had her spirit. What in the world did she mean? How could I have my grandmother's spirit? It was all a little eerie to me. But I did realize that I had been told a lot more than what I had convinced myself was important. I had always dismissed those "back then" conversations as having no influence on my life. Yes, I did have high cheekbones, dark hair, and dark skin from my grandmother, but I thought that was as far as the connection went.

As I finally approached the chest, a sense of awe came over me. I trembled when I reached to open it. It was as though I was opening something sacred. I've seen in movies what happens to people who raid tombs. I've read about illnesses that befall those who disturb sacred places and the dead. Was this going to be one of those instances? Would my aunt and Mom find me dead in the attic because I opened a sacred chest? My aunt had requested that I not remove anything. Was that the reason? Would a spirit follow me home if I disturbed my grandmother's special belongings?

I was scared to touch it, but I couldn't move my hand off it. It was as though there was a hand on top of mine that was pushing my fingers to unlatch the lock. My heart pounded; my eyes were filled with tears. What was going on? I was always in control and always knew what I wanted. I was a girl in control, not like my brother who did everything to please someone else.

Did I dare open that chest, or did I dare walk away? I knew there was no good answer. I knew that this moment would change me forever. It already had. Just being in this attic and in the presence of my grandmother, I knew I would never be the same. There, I had said it, "in the presence of my grandmother," and I was. I knew it; my heart knew it—every fiber of my being knew it.

Tears flowed down my cheeks. *Stop it!* I screamed! *What are you doing to yourself? You are in control! But you are losing it.* The silent sobs kept coming. I cried for everything wrong in my life. I cried for all of my fears and those that might have been shared by my grandmother. Then peace came over me. For in that thought, my grandmother gave me peace. If she had made it and lived a long life, then so could I. I had made my decision.

I slowly opened the chest, and there it was. There in full display were all the pieces that made my grandmother who she was. I slowly started to remove a small picture album when I heard my mother behind me.

"I see you've discovered our baby pictures. It's time to go. Maybe on our next visit to Aunt Sissy's you can take a look at those old pictures. You probably wouldn't recognize any of the people, maybe Aunt Sissy and me. Anyway, that was then, and this is now. They are just old photos of days gone by. Let's go."

I could not move even though my lips pushed out the words "Okay, I'll be right down." I could not move. The book that was burning my hands paralyzed me. Do I put it back, or do I sneak it with me? After all, it's just some old photos. I felt my grandmother's presence encouraging me to open the book, while my mother's voice called me to leave.

It seemed like an eternity to make the decision to place it back in the chest just as I had been directed to do. I didn't know if I was more scared of a bad spirit following me for doing wrong and removing something sacred or losing this moment with my grandmother. I knew one thing for sure. I would be returning to this attic and to the life my grandmother was so desperately trying to share with me.

"Well, Breeby, you are drenched! What did you discover up there? I thought I was going to have to go up there and get you. I was afraid you had passed out with heat exhaustion. You know that attic is over one hundred degrees on these hot summer days?"

Aunt Sissy was right about all of that. For the first time in my life, hearing her voice didn't make me want to cringe. Something had happened to me, and the scary part was I was not in control of it. Then I heard myself saying the unthinkable, "Mom, when can we visit Aunt Sissy again?" I thought they were going to flip out.

Mom's answer even startled me more. "Boy, I don't know what ghost you encountered up there, but we will have to see."

That was always her answer when she had no other answer. Today, that was not good enough. At the same time, I couldn't tell them about my attic experience. I didn't know how much of it was real and how much of it may have been related to being around old things in an exhaustingly hot attic. I would have to give this some deep thought.

As we backed out of the driveway, I found myself waving to Cooper. What was I doing? I was not in control of my actions. I hated the boy, yet there it was. My hand was up in the air, waving bye to my aunt's new neighbor. There he was, a neighbor that I detested, and yet I had this strange feeling of envy because he was moving in next door.

Chapter 2

For the next couple of days, I could think of nothing but the chest in the attic of my aunt's house. What was in it, and what was the story behind each item that seemed to have been so delicately placed in the chest?

I thought of Cooper. I thought of our first encounter and how he made me so mad. I didn't understand the thoughts that were taking over my rational mind. I was always in control. I never let anyone get the best of me. I was good at putting people in their places, especially know-it-all boys. I had experienced lots of practice at school, being the girl who was never chosen by anybody to be on any team.

I began searching our family albums for pictures of my grandmother. With each discovery came a flood of never-ending questions hijacking my thoughts. I slowly tried to stir my mom's memory so that I could piece together the life of a woman I never met. I searched on the computer for family names and places I knew they had lived. A computer search is a wonderful thing, but you have to be able to feed it some information for it to give up its secrets.

My mother soon took notice that I had changed my outlook on sleeping all day and talking with my friends on social media. She even commented at dinner one night that I appeared to be coming out of my cocoon. I could not believe she had said that in front of my brother, Matt, the perfect one.

"Who knows," she commented, "she might actually have some friends one day. We might see her want to look like a girl instead of a tomboy."

Just what did that mean? Was that not the same kind of nasty remark Cooper said his friends in Atlanta had said about girls in the south? For once, even though I gritted my teeth at the comment, I truly didn't care. I was on a mission. She could call it whatever she wanted to. I knew that she would never understand, with her attitude of my inability to do anything right. Anyway, I was not going to be limited by her view of me. I was going to do what I had purposed in my heart to do. I needed to get back to my aunt's house.

July Fourth weekend was soon approaching. Like everything else the pandemic had stolen, it was also stealing all the fun I usually had on the Fourth of July. My scheme was quickly taking shape. I would ask my parents if we could go to my aunt's house to celebrate since we could not have our typical celebration on the beach. It was a perfect idea. Because we were all family, and it would be a limited number of people, a celebration at my aunt's would be perfect. It didn't hurt either that she and my uncle always had food that I liked to eat. While my aunt was a health nut, she did remember what it was like to be a teenager.

When I sold the idea to Mom and Dad, they quickly got on board. There was just one small problem. My brother would already have something planned, and he always got what he wanted. His plans never included all of us. We just had to stay home in case something happened or if Matt's plans changed. So Mom and Dad would allow him to go to his best friend's house for a pool party and cookout. Mom and I were never allowed to do our own thing on holidays. My dad always insisted, "The family has to play together." He never realized that his "playing together" was always torture for me.

As we packed the car, I was elated. I was still in disbelief that my father had agreed to my brother's little scheme and mine as well. It was going to finally be a good holiday. I tried to contain my excitement for the trip that lay ahead. I was going to my aunt's, but better than that, I would find a way to return to the attic.

I was quiet during the hour's drive north. I had to come up with a really good reason why I needed to get into that attic. It was a hot July day in South Georgia. The attic would be unbearable, but I didn't care. I dressed in summer clothes, and I would take bottles of water to the attic with me. That was the easy part. Convincing my parents on why I had a need to go up into the attic was a different story.

At some point, my mother's words ripped through my thoughts. "Well, Abreea, it looks like Cooper's house is finished. I wonder if they have moved in, and if so, if they will be at Aunt Sissy's cookout today?"

Oh no, I had not even remotely thought of that possibility or interference. I would not be allowed to leave him since I was the only person who would be attending the cookout who would be his age. And I surely was not going to be allowed to take him to the attic, nor did I want to. That attic was mine. What was in that attic was mine, mine alone, not to be shared with anyone. Suddenly, I felt sick on my stomach. Once again, he had robbed me of my joy, my time. I just didn't like him. Why couldn't he just leave me alone? I suddenly remembered the wave. I had actually waved bye to him as we left my aunt's house on our last visit.

As soon as we arrived at my aunt's house, Uncle Joe whisked me away to go crabbing with him on their dock. I loved my uncle. He was the only member of our family who seemed to understand me and to rescue me when other adults appeared to be pressuring me. I have never figured out if it's intentional or if he does all kids that way. Today, I didn't care. I would think about that at another time.

I love to catch crabs in mesh baskets. Crabs look like prehistoric creatures. The way they run sideways is messed up. It's straight from some outer planet movie scheme. I also like to turn them over and rub their stomachs to put them to sleep. The trick is to know how to pick them up so you can flip them over.

We had only been crabbing a few minutes when I looked down the pier to see Cooper and a man I guessed was his father walking toward us. My nightmare was quickly coming true. Once again, Cooper would ruin everything just like he had on our first encounter. To make matters worse, I knew I would officially be on babysitting duty. It also meant that I would never make it to the attic. Once again, the adults had not bothered to ask me how I felt about the situation. In fact, they never asked me anything. They just assumed that their ideas would just be great for me. I would be expected to babysit this jerk all day long.

So I did what I knew best to do. I quickly pulled up another crab, and boy was he huge! I accidentally dumped him on the dock, narrowly missing the bucket of water. I quickly shrieked like a girl, and Cooper did what I knew he would do.

Sure enough, this tough guy from Atlanta reached down to pick it up to show me who was the best. It couldn't have happened better in the movies. That crab clamped his jaw on the jerk's finger. The more Cooper slung his hand trying to get him off, the more the crab hung on, and the more I laughed. Cooper was screaming and crying like a girl.

Of course, I knew I would be in trouble because my uncle knew I was a better crabber than that. I seldom missed the bucket. On the few occasions when I did, I knew how to reach down and carefully grab the crab by his two back legs. I usually turned him over and put him to sleep by rubbing his stomach.

With the crying and screaming to get the crab off his finger, I knew I would have to explain my laughter. I tried to tell my uncle that I didn't make Cooper pick the crab up. It wasn't my fault that he didn't know better. My uncle asked me to apologize for the laughter. I had to force the words out of my mouth. But just as soon as I turned to run up the pier, I had a skip in my step and a song on my lips. I had won. Cooper had robbed me of my time with my uncle, but it cost him a sore finger and wounded pride of knowing that I had seen him cry.

The rest of the boring day was uneventful. I was constantly planning and scheming on how I could get into the attic. Finally, I just decided to ask my aunt about the items in my grandmother's chest. She was of no help. All she could recall were pictures, some little trinkets of my mom's and hers when they were growing up, and possibly a couple of old letters from relatives that her mom had kept. "Nothing of any importance."

"Well, would you mind if I looked through it?"

"Breeby, it's too hot up there today. Maybe next time."

"Please, I'm bored and don't want to listen to y'all talk, and I surely don't want to hang around with Cooper."

"Ask your mom, maybe fifteen minutes."

As I scampered up the stairs to the attic, I could barely contain my excitement. I couldn't believe I had actually made it back to the place that had been burning in my memory for weeks. I quickly realized that I felt dizzy, light-headed. Then I thought my heart was going to beat out of my chest. My hands began to sweat. I had to calm down. There was obviously something in that attic that controlled me.

I sat on the floor in front of the chest, hesitant to open it. This time I was not going to use my precious fifteen minutes touching and thinking about all of the old items stored up there. I would return to those thoughts on another day.

Slowly, I lifted the lid. It was as though I was being told what to do, which item to pick up first. Just as my aunt had said, I could see an old family picture album, some trinkets from their childhood, and some baby clothes. But my aunt had said something about old letters. Old letters that I could not see added to my anxiety. Did those letters contain a secret that had been sealed with my grandmother's death? Was it meant to stay locked away through the passage of time?

My aunt's request had remained the same. I could enjoy myself with two conditions: I could not remove anything from the attic, and I had to place the items back in the chest the way I found them. Well, that would be easy. I would just take pictures with my phone. Where was my phone? Oh no, I had left my phone in the car when my uncle had quickly whisked me away to fish for crabs on the dock.

I speedily made a mad dash down the stairs to have Mom tell me that my dad and uncle had taken our car to town to buy toppings for the homemade ice cream. So I rapidly returned to the attic. I had only been up there for what seemed like a few minutes when Mom called me down for ice cream and fireworks. Reluctantly, I returned the picture album to its rightful place in the chest. I could not return the images; they were forever embedded in my brain.

After pictures of my mom and aunt as babies and special events while they were growing up had been a picture of me. I gasped when

I first turned the page and saw someone who looked just like me staring back through the pages of time. I felt faint. I was much older and wearing some funky clothes, but there I was! Is it possible that I really do have my grandmother's spirit, or did it mean that my spirit was just like that of my grandmother? I knew that this moment had changed my life. It had changed my way of thinking, my way of looking at the world, and my life. Would I ever know again which decisions were truly mine or which decisions were being made for me by a person's spirit whom I had never met? I knew I would spend my life searching for those answers.

I was snapped back to reality when Mom called a second time, "Abreea Louise, you have to come down. I don't know what has your attention so well, but you've been up there for an hour."

I couldn't move, not because I had passed out. I could not force myself to leave my grandmother in the attic. Quickly, I turned to see my mother standing over me.

"Are you okay? Look, you are soaked! You are dehydrated. You look as though you've seen a ghost! This heat has gotten to you. Let me help you down."

I didn't need help getting down the stairs. I didn't need water, and I definitely didn't need ice cream. I just needed to be left alone in that attic to meet the person who had given me her spirit. I needed my grandmother! With my mother tugging at my arm, I slowly teetered my way to standing.

"Honey, you can't come up here anymore in this heat. It is making you sick."

How could I tell her I was not sick? How could I tell her that the heat had nothing to do with the way I looked? I had to tell her something that would allow me a return trip back into the attic. How do you tell someone that your life has been changed forever at the ripe old age of thirteen? And worse yet, did I even want to tell her? This was my secret, my grandmother's and mine.

The ice cream and fireworks were uneventful. The drive home wasn't much better. I needed to get to my room. I had held an image in my head that I had to get on paper before all the chatter from the adults faded my memory away. I didn't want to forget even one frown line.

My hand couldn't draw fast enough. What soon emerged was a likeness of the person from the picture in the attic. What story was behind those big almond-shaped eyes? I knew there was a connection to me, but what? How was I ever going to get my answers when Mom rarely spoke of her childhood, and I seldom visited Aunt Sissy?

Chapter 3

As the weeks of summer slid away like a thief who steals just enough to make you angry, it took the image of the attic pictures with it. Mom and Dad were busy working from home as demanded by the pandemic. We seldom went anywhere, not even to church. My brother was busy doing his own thing of working at the pharmacy, delivering meds to elderly people. I was, for once in my life, left alone to do whatever I wanted.

A few short months ago, I would have longed for this opportunity, but that was then. Now I found myself wanting adult conversation about earlier years. I wanted to hear about the years my parents describe as a time when everything was nicer: no pandemic, people loved each other, God, and country. Where had that peaceful time gone? All I really wanted were a few answers to some simple questions.

As the talk of school returned, I was in for another shock. No face-to-face and no football games. Learning would be virtual. My world had fallen apart. I could not imagine having to share my classroom with my mother, father, and older brother. There would be no privacy.

This was the year I was finally going to "be somebody." I had gotten a little taller and was beginning to look more like a girl instead of a lanky boy. Maybe I had even become a little prettier, or so I thought. This was the year I was going to join clubs and go to football games. I was no longer going to be that cute, sweet, smart girl who could draw but was not accepted into "the crowd." I had never been popular like my brother. In fact, I was the total opposite of my brother, and everyone loved to remind me of that.

The only thing that appeared to be mine and mine alone was whatever was in that chest in that attic. Like me, it was tucked away where it didn't cause trouble. Yet if it was ever needed, it could be pulled out and dusted off. Other than that, it had little value.

As I sat in my room drawing, my mother came in with the laundry. "Oh, Breeby, that is a really good drawing. I've never seen you draw a self-portrait. You should frame that and put it on your wall."

A chill ran down my spine, and I shivered. I quickly returned to the feelings I had experienced when I visited the attic, but this time I was in my bedroom. That picture was not of me; it was of my grandmother! My mother had not even noticed.

As I gazed at my drawing, my eyes trailed up to the girl in the mirror. I was transfixed. I recognized the face, but I didn't know the girl at all. Those were not my eyes staring back at me. Had my grandmother's spirit taken over my life, or had I stolen her identity?

I don't know how many hours I had been sleeping when a loud clap of thunder jarred me from my bed. The drawing had been lying beside me and fell to the floor with the sudden jump. I bent down to pick it up and realized how bad my head ached. In fact, it wasn't just my head; my whole body ached, including my heart and soul. It was 2:00 a.m. I couldn't go to the kitchen for fear of waking my parents. I couldn't take a shower either. I heard the rain falling gently on my windowpane. So I just decided to open my curtains, lie in bed, and watch it rain. I wondered, *Had my grandmother ever found herself in a similar situation. Was this unique to me or had she been here before?* I wondered a lot of things about my grandmother.

As I wandered into the kitchen the next morning for breakfast, I heard my parents talking about a tropical depression that had the potential of building into a hurricane within the next two weeks. They were also talking about my father's next job excursion. Since my father worked with Homeland Security, he was frequently away on trips and could not share his information or destination with us. This was one of those trips. A hurricane without my father would be just one more thing I did not need in my life. It meant that my brother and I would have to help Mom prepare for the hurricane.

As we went through the next couple of days, my attention was taken away from the drawing and the woman in the attic. I was getting ready to return to school online. That meant no new clothes and no new excitement. We had finished last year online, and it was not fun. It also meant that my schoolwork would have to have my attention.

The storm in the Atlantic Ocean had continued to gain strength and was now a hurricane. Since it had a small chance of hitting Jacksonville, this made my mom go crazy. Her focus was turned immediately to not having electricity after the storm. There were all the extra chores of making sure clothes were washed and put away. We had to have extra meals cooked and frozen. There was my job of making sure all the extra space in the freezer contained a bag of water to be frozen, but I couldn't just fill it up at one time. There was something in Mom's head about taxing the freezer, whatever that means. Mom also had to make sure that all of our medicines were in abundant supply. Then there was the grocery shopping for groceries like Spam and cans of pork 'n beans, food we only eat when there is going to be a storm. I didn't like Spam on a good day. I couldn't believe she would feed that to us on a hot, bad day with no electricity.

As the storm approached, the chores were redirected to include moving flowerpots and other yard objects that could be picked up by the wind. Patio furniture had to be tied up or brought inside. My brother and I had to walk around outside and pretend the wind could make missiles out of pots and chairs. That was how we determined what was moved or tied down. We both knew the potential disaster that could be caused by winds in a hurricane. Even if the storm didn't hit us directly, Dad and Mom always took us to help neighboring cities clean up after a hurricane passed through.

As the hurricane grew closer, it was determined that the storm would directly hit Northeast Florida. After all of that work to get ready for the storm, my dad told my mom to take us to Aunt Sissy's. He did not want us to be alone, and Uncle Joe would be there to help if needed.

So Mom packed the car with the extra food she had purchased and clothes for us to wear. She bathed our dog Jack and put him in the back seat with me. I loved that dog, but I detested his slobber all over me. Anyway, we pulled away from our home with heavy hearts. I loved living there. I loved the salt air, the sand between my toes, the marsh grasses, the many kinds of birds, and the stars at night. I prayed I was not seeing it for the last time.

I soon got lost in the hum of the car's engine and dozed off to sleep. When I awoke, we were pulling into my aunt's driveway. It hit me between the eyes. I was going to spend an unknown number of days with my aunt Sissy at her house, the house with the attic with its secrets of my grandmother. I was elated!

As we moved our luggage and food into my aunt's house, there was an eerie calm in the air. The typical ocean breeze was still, and the skies were gray. Mom said we would get a lot of rain, but not the damaging winds. I was okay with a few rainy days. The attic would be cooler, and they would have no excuse for not letting me spend time in the chest.

As I went to bed, I realized the room I was sharing with my mom was directly under the place in the attic where my grandmother's spirit slept in that old chest. I also looked out the window through the drizzling rain toward the new house next door. I was looking at the soft light that was escaping through drawn curtains into the bedroom that would be Cooper's. I wondered if this was his first hurricane and if he was scared. I wondered if his dad would comfort him like Mom was comforting me. I also realized that this moment was like the time when I had waved bye to him. I felt sympathy and not hate. I would keep that little tidbit of information to myself. Was this the real me, or was this the spirit of my grandmother creeping into my inner soul? With that thought tucked in tight, I went to sleep.

Chapter 4

I heard the murmuring of the adults downstairs with the TV softly playing in the background. What time was it anyway? It was still dark outside. As I crept down the stairs, I heard the meteorologist say that the storm had wobbled and shifted directions. It was headed straight our way, and it was too late to leave. Where would we go? All inland hotels were filled with people from Florida, and it was already too dangerous to drive. We couldn't take the chance of running out of gas or, worse, having to ride the storm out in the car parked in a parking lot at some unknown location.

The governor was telling people to shelter in place. I quickly forgot all about the things that had consumed me for months. My heart was pounding. This was serious, and I knew my mother would be frantic to protect all of us. Mom was not the "cool" one. All of the calmness genes had been given to Aunt Sissy. I knew my father would try to get back to us in the storm. I also knew that my life could change yet again forever. I had so much to think about, I had to remind myself to breathe.

Planning and preparing once again to get through this storm followed a quick breakfast. Mom ran to the grocery for whatever supplies were still available. My uncle and brother started boarding up the windows. My job was to help Aunt Sissy move outdoor furniture and flowerpots. This was becoming a nightmare with each passing hour. We had just spent three days at home doing the same thing. Now we didn't have three days to prepare. We had today, and we had each other.

After hours of working, Uncle Joe announced that Cooper's dad might need some help since he had never been through this kind of storm. So everyone jumped in to put boards on windows and tie down all the outside furniture. As we turned to go home, Aunt Sissy did the unthinkable. She invited Cooper and his dad to ride the storm out with all of us at her house. She had the extra room, and with today's prep, she had extra supplies. I was so thankful when Cooper's dad said they would be okay. Their new house was built to withstand hurricanes, and they would be just fine.

I awoke early to the sound of rain beating against the window-pane. I realized that Mom was not in bed. In fact, I don't think she had been in bed all night. The sheets and blankets were just as I had left them when I finally went to sleep. I knew we were as prepared as we could be. Aunt Sissy had taken charge, making sure that every-body and everything was in its place. At the last minute, the governor of Georgia mandated that everyone who lived east of I-95 evacuate and go further inland. My aunt lives two miles west of that zone. My brilliant uncle and mother wanted to ride it out, arguing that it would be more dangerous to leave. How stupid could two adults be, but there we were. Aunt Sissy had surrendered all her power to leave the day before, but those two were going to stay. That meant we all had to stay. Yet once again, they didn't ask for my opinion.

I quickly slid into an old pair of jeans and a baggy shirt, the kind of clothes you lay around in when you are sick. While I wasn't physically sick, I was sick in some sort of way. I was sick of this situation. I was sick that Cooper had been invited to stay. I wondered if he was downstairs, but then I didn't really want to know that answer either. I was sick that I would have to hear how great my uncle is about everything. Even though I really like him, I do get tired of his boasting all the time. Not only does he know everything, but he has also been everywhere and done everything. I was sick that my dad was not with us. I often wondered what he does on his job and if he is safe.

I really wondered if I would make it to the attic. I knew that yesterday was not a good time to ask. I had looked forward to coming to my aunt's when I thought the storm was headed somewhere else. I thought that I would have a couple of days to find my way through all the stuff up in the attic. I could not have been more wrong. With that storm headed this way, I knew my place, up to now, was to help prepare for this storm without asking questions and being a nuisance. I was sick of so many things, but most of all, I was sick of not knowing who I am, not knowing me. I truly believe that answer is in the attic in the chest directly over my room.

As the morning before, I crept down the stairs as though I were a cat trying to hide from my dog, Jack. The mood in the kitchen was somber, people talking in whispers. Since most windows were covered with boards, it gave the impression that we were hiding from the world. That was too much like my reality. I had hidden from the world for years. I felt safer that way. People couldn't hurt me if I didn't let them into my inner thoughts. This time, it didn't feel safer. I wanted to see outside. I wanted to know how my world was changing and how I was going to fit into that new world.

Aunt Sissy was making pancakes for anybody who wanted to eat. She was pretty much ignored as everybody was glued to the TV in the next room. The report was not good. The only hope was that the storm would wobble east and not grow stronger.

Most of that day was spent watching TV while waiting for the next rain band to come through. When there was a break in the storm, we would run outside and down to the dock. One thing was happening for sure; the water was getting higher and closer to reaching the planks on the dock and pier.

The adults started talking about the storm surge. I had heard that term in science class, but I had never thought much about it. In previous years, I would hear about all the damage and deaths that were caused by the storm surge. I never understood it. Why didn't people just get out of the way? Now I hear the adults talking about the water rising high enough to float my uncle's new dock and pier out to the ocean. They also talked about the water rising high enough to get into the house. I knew this was serious. My aunt's house sets high on a bluff overlooking the saltwater marsh and creek that meanders to the river. At high tide, you can even see the river that runs straight to the ocean. The more they talked, the more I missed my father. He could make everything all right.

The rainbands were coming more frequent now and with stronger winds and more sideways rain. We could no longer venture outside. Uncle Joe had left one small window facing the marsh uncovered. He wanted to be able to see what was happening to his dock. The meteorologist had predicted that we would get the worst of the storm during the night and the next morning. As the evening wore on, we were getting news reports of trees falling on houses and thousands of people in Florida without power.

The first tree fell just before dark, and my uncle and Mom screamed like girls. Aunt Sissy and I had been standing behind Mom who was seated on the sofa facing the marsh and the only uncovered window. It was like a scene from an old movie where everything happened in slow motion. We all watched in disbelief as a huge live oak on the edge of the bluff fell straight toward the house and the room where we were. I was horrified! About ten minutes earlier, I had hurriedly taken Jack outside in the wind and rain to take care of his business in that exact spot. Mom brought me back to reality when she asked Uncle Joe if they had life preservers.

Aunt Sissy just casually replied, "We do. They are downstairs in the closet in the garage, but I don't think a life jacket will save you now." She turned and walked away.

Within ten minutes, everything went dead. There was absolutely no sound in the house, and there were no lights. It was getting dark and in a hurry. It was as though we had stolen from the darkness so long that it was quickly reclaiming its territory, and it was winning.

Aunt Sissy said, "This is it. Hunker down. We'll all be okay."

A few hours earlier, she had made all of us put a small flashlight in our pockets. At the time she handed one to me, I thought it was one of the dumbest, strangest things she had ever done. Now I was so thankful that she is a little kooky.

About that time, we heard a pounding on the front door. Jack and Aunt Sissy's dog, Mr. Squiggles, went crazy! Uncle Joe opened it to find Cooper and his dad standing there huddled together. They were drenched and scared to death! All they had with them was a plastic grocery bag containing a changing of clothes and a box of

Goldfish. How weird! I had my answer to an earlier thought. That know-it-all tough guy and his dad did not know how to prepare for a hurricane.

Cooper said the trees looked like they were being beaten. He said he and his father had been scared to run the two lots to our house. The trees were doubled over like they were throwing up. Limbs and debris were flying everywhere, and the wind was so strong his daddy had to literally hold on to him, or he would have been blown away.

At that moment, I felt truly sorry for him. Where was his mother? He needed her to comfort him. I was so thankful that Mom and Aunt Sissy had prepared. They both knew exactly what to do for such a time as this.

Aunt Sissy ushered Cooper and his dad into a bedroom while handing them their flashlights. I kind of snickered as I wondered if Cooper thought she was weird or was he already past that to the thankful stage. She told them to get dry and join the family downstairs.

Aunt Sissy had prepared a room on the bottom floor of her three-story house that she deemed "the safe room." Her belief was that it would be the safest room in the house and could withstand the deadly wind and trees that were hurling outside. Their house had been built to new building codes that included strict hurricane guidelines, but the house had never been tested.

They soon joined us in the storm room. Aunt Sissy gave them the same orders she had given us. We were to stay in this room, stay away from the three covered windows, limit the use of cell phones and computers, and look out after each other. We all knew we were in for a long, hot night. We couldn't open windows and without electricity, there was no air conditioning or even fans.

I was thankful that the storm room was huge. It was typically used as a gym and Uncle Joe's office. It was large enough that we could somewhat spread out, but we couldn't get away from that obnoxious weather radio. It was constantly sounding dreadful bad weather alerts. We knew it was bad weather; we didn't need anyone to tell us that information. Even so, all we could really hear was the deafening sound of the howling wind.

As we found our places, my thoughts turned to the people in the room. I wondered if all of them had been mixed up when they were in middle school. Had bullies made fun of them? Even worse, had people they called friends turned on them? Had adults made decisions about them without including them? As I looked at each of them individually, I started making up their stories based on what little I actually knew about them. My aunt and uncle had probably met on some exotic island. Cooper's dad was probably a world traveler. Then for the first time, I wondered about Cooper's mom. How could a mother go away and just leave her only child with his father? One day I would ask Cooper about that, but tonight was not the right time.

I allowed myself to play a card game with Cooper, and of course, he cheated to win. I just let it pass. I expected as much. I had already summed him up to be that kind of guy. He was just like all the guys that had been in my classes last year at my school. I thought of how this situation was like camping out. Instead of a firelight, we had flashlights. Instead of sleeping bags on the ground, we had all been assigned a cot, lounger, or air mattress on the floor. Then it hit me! I had to sleep in the same room with Cooper! Somehow, after the danger was gone, he would use that against me when talking with his city friends.

I was rescued from that thought by the tornado alert that was blasting through the airwaves. Where were we going to go? We were already in the safest room of the house. Aunt Sissy said we would have to get in the storage closet under the stairwell and put our pillows over our heads. This was one thing Cooper and I agreed upon. We knew the drill because we had both practiced it so many times at school. We neither one thought we would ever use it.

As we sat in silence waiting for the house to cave in on us or for the top two floors to be blown away, we were all in our own thoughts or saying our prayers. What seemed like an eternity ended when the meteorologists said that the tornado had moved into the neighboring county. We been spared that time, but we weren't sure about the top of the house or Cooper's home.

We gradually settled back down in the storm room and tried to play board games or cards, but our hearts were not in them. Something had changed while huddled in that small closet, and it had changed for all of us. I finally dozed off and was then suddenly awakened by it, that awful weather alert signaling that tornadoes were in our area. I felt as though I was one of those stuffed animals in a carnival game with people throwing balls trying to knock me off my pedestal. Just like those ugly, stupid animals, I was thankfully still sitting in my spot waiting for the next jerk to show his strength to a girl by winning her a large stuffed animal.

As the dawn started breaking, we could see through the cracks of space around one of the windows. Water and limbs and fallen trees were everywhere. The wind and rain continued with a vengeance. They kept pounding and knocking limbs and trees over. They had not caused enough pain. Uncle Joe announced that we should stay in the storm room until the wind and rain stopped. It didn't take us long that morning to realize how the heat had crept in and was now going to make us miserable. Uncle Joe had a generator but couldn't run it until the rain completely stopped.

Aunt Sissy had prepared a basket of pop tarts and pastries that could be eaten for breakfast. A cooler of chilled Cokes was our morning beverage. It was so refreshing, almost like a commercial. We were in the middle of a storm, and yet we were smiling and giddy over a cold Coke. As we ate, Uncle Joe said it was almost over. We had made it through the night and the worst of it. He did not know the condition of the house but was thankful that the storm room had lived up to its promises. We were safe.

Uncle Joe quickly reminded us that it would be unsafe to venture outdoors even after the worst of the storm had passed. The trees and limbs had taken a beating last night and might still be fragile. He told us that it would not take much wind to topple a tree or to blow a broken limb down out of one. He pleaded with us to be cautious for the next couple of days and weeks to come. The neighborhood was built under huge oaks, and everybody who lived there were tree huggers, meaning that residents didn't remove trees even when they had been told by an arborist to do so.

Around ten that morning, Uncle Joe and Cooper's dad ventured to the top two floors, requesting that we stay behind. They were afraid that we would get cut on broken glass and dangling rafters. The two of them tiptoed up the stairs, expecting the roof to be gone or walls to be missing. I wondered about my chest in the attic, if the attic was even still there. Shortly, he yelled that it was all clear, so we raced up the stairs. It was as if we had been set free from a cage.

We found the house still intact, no broken windows or gaping holes in the ceiling, no trees in the den. We raced to look out the den window that Uncle Joe had not boarded up. The ocean was in the backyard! We were all in disbelief at the amount of water that covered the marsh grass and most of Uncle Joe's pier. We could barely see the blades of marsh grass peeping through the lake of water. The place was a mess!

While the excitement of going outside ran through our veins, the anticipation of what we might find was written on our faces. The fear of the unknown had been my constant companion this past year, but I had never seen it on adults' faces until this moment.

Uncle Joe slightly opened the door to survey the damage and to let the dogs out. Huge trees were lying in a circle all around the house. It looked like someone had played dominoes with the trees and knocked them all over. We were all in awe. How did all of those trees fall without any of us feeling the house shake or hearing them hit the ground? We hadn't all been asleep at the same time, or asleep at all. The house had been eerily quiet with the occasional exception of our whispering or munching on Cooper's Goldfish. The sound the angry winds made as they howled around the house had been deafening. It was as though the storm was punishing us for building the house on its bluff.

The rain suddenly and finally stopped. Uncle Joe declared it would soon be safe to venture out. He once again alerted us to all the hidden dangers. We had come through the storm, but there was still a storm in the trees. He also reminded us that snakes and other animals had been run out of their homes and maybe hiding in different places in our yards and neighborhood. He also told us that the saltwater would quickly return to the ocean and that we shouldn't be on the edge of the bluff or go on the pier or dock. I was just glad to know that we had made it this far.

By lunch, Uncle Joe gave us permission to cautiously venture outside. While standing in the front yard glaring at the root ball of a huge oak, he reminded us that the wind would likely continue to gust for an hour or so. He also told us to be aware of falling trees and limbs that were just waiting to come down. He had barely gotten the words out of his mouth when a huge water oak fell three feet in front of us. It was as if the tree obeyed his words to teach us a lesson. Lesson learned, and I would never forget it!

Our first cautious task was to check on all of the neighbors. At first glance, we noticed devastation everywhere in the neighborhood, but all the houses were still standing. Some houses, including Cooper's, had suffered broken windows and flooding rain that had blown into the house, but all of the people were okay.

The next task was to begin the cleanup. The sun had come back with a vengeance. The wind had completely stopped. It was ninety-eight degrees, and flying bugs were everywhere! Bugs I had never seen before. Uncle Joe said the storm might have actually blown some of them out of their habitats and into ours. That was just what we needed, more stinging, biting bugs.

For the first time since the storm passed, I looked up at the attic. It had been spared, along with my grandmother's secrets. Not having time to think about the attic, or me, I began helping Cooper haul tree limbs to the street. One huge tree had fallen across the driveway. It had to be removed before anything else could be done. We had to be able to leave the house, and the men were anxious to do so. I didn't understand exactly where the men were going to go because trees were everywhere.

As I worked, I thought about my last year's teacher encouraging us to keep a diary. If I had done so, what would I say about all of this? What would my entry be today? I already knew that, once again, I was changing. I didn't know how, and I surely didn't know why. I just knew that this was one more thing, another piece of this year that had changed me forever.

Chapter 5

Uncle Joe pushed the starter on the generator, and it cranked right up. The sound of the motor was heaven. It meant that we could take a warm bath and sleep in an air-conditioned room tonight. Mom and Aunt Sissy prepared lunch and served us as though it had been a Fourth of July celebration. It was a celebration! It was a celebration of being alive and of a house that had stood the wrath of Mother Nature. It had kept us safe, and it had also saved the secrets in the attic.

While eating, we heard on the radio that a lot of people had gotten stranded on the interstate when the storm changed direction. They ran out of gas, and hotels were closed.

As soon as lunch was over, and our driveway was cleared, Aunt Sissy and Mom decided to see if there were any people stranded at our exit. They loaded the Jeep with water and sandwiches. They weren't gone very long when they came back with stories of just how many people were stranded in this heat. The roads were closed because of trees, debris and, in some places, downed power lines. At one point, Mom and Aunt Sissy allowed a single mom and two small kids with medical problems to use the downstairs bathroom. It was something I had never seen. Total strangers were helping each other, allowing kids to use our bathroom amid a pandemic. Mom was quick to hand out masks.

Cooper and I had taken a break from hauling limbs and sat in the swing that overlooked the marsh and US 17. We could see blue lights from cop cars and were very curious as to why they were stopped at the bridge's edge. My uncle and brother decided to ride down to the bridge to see if they could help. They thought someone might have gone into the river during the storm. When they returned, they told us that there was so much devastation that looters were walking into homes that had been evacuated and were stealing anything of value. The governor had placed armed military guards on the other side of the bridge that separated us from the next county. They were not letting people cross the bridge into that county unless they could prove to be residents. Also, due to the number of trees down across the road, it was unsafe to drive.

This was what I had imagined it might be like to live in those countries where war was always going on, but this was America, and we were not at war with another country. We had been at war with Mother Nature, and she had won.

As Cooper and I sat in the swing, we started talking about the events from last night. Neither of us could believe that seven huge trees had fallen in a circle around my aunt's house, and the only damage to the house was the two shingles that had blown off the roof. We also could not believe that we didn't hear the trees groaning as they were violently jerked from the earth. Neither were there any vibrations from the anguish of the limbs crushing and hitting the ground. We were in total disbelief.

As we had walked around the neighborhood earlier checking on our neighbors, we saw the devastation on two wooded lots four blocks down on either side of my aunt's house. Last night, the meteorologists had warned us about a tornado that was hitting our neighborhood. It had toppled every huge tree on those lots. It looked like the domino effect when you push over a long line of dominoes. It had also taken the tops out of most of the trees in Aunt Sissy's yard and in Cooper's yard.

The new house being constructed next to Cooper's had a tiny limb jammed through the ceiling. It was like a science experiment of sticking a straw through a raw potato. You could see the limb dangling like a javelin in the unfinished master bedroom. I knew this moment would live forever in my memory. I knew that it had changed me; I just didn't know how.

We continued to just sit and slightly move the swing to keep the bugs from making us their evening meal. It was getting late, but there was limited power even with the generator, so there was no need to rush inside. That power was saved for the refrigerators, freezers, and light cooking. Uncle Joe had said that we would turn the air on in the "safe room" to sleep since it had its own air-conditioning unit. That meant that I was going to have to spend a second night with Cooper.

Uncle Joe had also said that while he had extra cans of gas, that it may be days or weeks before we could buy more. He also believed it would take weeks for the power companies to repair all of the downed power lines to restore our energy. I was so thankful for not having any worse damage, but I quickly became consumed by the emotions that were now creeping back into my thoughts. We still had not heard from our father, nor had I heard from my friends in my neighborhood in White Sand Beach.

Cooper interrupted my thoughts. He was talking in such a low voice that I wasn't sure if he was speaking or thinking out loud.

"I was really scared last night. I've never been through anything like that. Your aunt Sissy reminds me of my mother. She would have been prepared for this storm. My daddy just didn't think it would be very bad. He had lived through several blizzards as a child. He said we would be okay if we just stayed inside away from the windows and watched TV. He had said that "it would be like a father-and-son camping party."

I didn't know whether to ask questions or just to listen. I thought I saw a tear roll down his cheek as he talked about his mother, but I would not dare turn to look at him. I realized that he was consumed with fears, emotions, and thoughts just like I was. I also knew at that moment that he was lost as well. He did not know who he was any more than I know who I am. Then I thought about the attic. I would find my answers in the attic, but where was he going to find his answers. All he knew was that living with Mom and Dad had never been pleasant.

His mom's job required that she travel internationally all the time. He and his dad had spent many weeks alone. When his mom was home, she had little time for them. She was always on the phone with clients or meeting clients for dinner. That meant that she seldom had dinner with them as a family. His father resented that she was the more successful of them. He resented that she traveled the world and left him behind to take care of Cooper. There was the sting; tears were now flowing freely down his cheeks. He loved his mother, and surely she loved him, but his dad never missed the opportunity to point out every occasion that she had abandoned them. He was abandoned!

That was one thing I was not. My father traveled but smothered me with his attention when he was home. He was always sending me pictures of beautiful nature scenes, and he always brought me little bracelets from his travels.

I had gotten so consumed in my own thoughts that I wasn't sure when he started talking about his fears for the upcoming school year. He was a new kid in a new grade, and he did not know anyone. To make matters worse, he would not be starting school in a building but virtually due to the pandemic.

Middle school was hard enough on the best of days. I had struggled last year, and I knew what he was facing. He would never fit into the popular circle of friends, and if he didn't get accepted into that group, that group would make his life miserable.

They were just like his father. They would not miss an opportunity to remind him of his misfits and mishaps. Adults believe they have bullying under control, but there is always a way for the devil to do his deeds. The devil lives in middle school. He had made my life miserable last year, and now he was working to do the same with Cooper's.

Why don't adults get it? Is there an unwritten law that middle-aged kids can't talk with adults? Does it state that these kids have to be spoken to, looked down on, and considered to be empty-headed of any good thoughts? I just don't get it, and now I know that Cooper doesn't get it either.

The day had slipped away, and I still had not made it to the attic. My emotions were more mixed up than ever. I felt sorry for Cooper, but I didn't need him. I didn't even really like him. I felt sorry for him, and feeling sorry for him was not going to help me with my issues. Somehow, he would have to figure out his own problems without my help. He could not know about the attic, nor that my answers were up there waiting for me.

The steam of the day had been replaced by the bugs of the night. We had not even noticed that darkness had fallen. There must have been a million stars twinkling in the sky. It's funny how we had never noticed them before. Neighborhood streetlights normally limited our view of the show that was taking place overhead. We started looking for the North Star and the Big Dipper. We had both studied the night sky since kindergarten, yet we were shocked how little we actually knew about the world that danced above us. We both vowed that we would learn the stars if we ever got back to our phones and computers.

We remembered that we hadn't eaten dinner, so we jumped out of the swing and raced to the kitchen. Mom was telling Aunt Sissy that Dad had called and would be home the next day. A few planes would be allowed to land at the Jacksonville airport, and he had booked a flight.

Dad said that he had a neighbor to check on our house in White Sand. We still didn't have power, and trees were everywhere, but he could run the basics on our generator. A1A and I-95 were open from Aunt Sissy's house to White Sand, so we would be going home in the morning.

I was a mental wreck again. I had to get to that chest. I did not know when I would be back to Aunt Sissy's, and my chances had faded once again. I had spent too much time with Cooper in that swing listening to his sad story and watching him cry.

Uncle Joe and Cooper's dad yelled that the hamburgers were ready. I could barely eat. Every time I took a bite of my hamburger, bugs took a bite of me. At least I learned that Cooper would be going home.

Tonight, we were sleeping in our own bedrooms. I needed some time alone. I had a lot of information and emotions to figure out. I had surprised myself today at some of the thoughts and emotions I had felt. Who am I? What kind of person am I? Am I just like the other kids in school whom I detested? Was I like some of the adults in my life that drove me insane with their comments and questions?

I went to sleep listening to the ticking in the ceiling fan. It was hot, but it was better than the cots in the air-conditioned "safe room."

The next morning was a scurry with Mom getting the car packed and Aunt Sissy cooking breakfast. As Mom helped Aunt Sissy clean the kitchen, Aunt Sissy told her that my brother and I could stay with them for a few days while she and Dad got our home back in shape. She then added that I would be a comfort to Cooper since he would be alone. My brother said he would be needed at home to help Daddy clear our yard and to help our neighbors clear theirs. It was settled that I would stay with Aunt Sissy. I had to mask the relief that was surely written all over my face, not that I wanted to stay because I liked Aunt Sissy that much. I did like that she had a chest in the attic that was calling for my attention, and I was ready to listen. It would not be pleasant having to see Cooper every day, but it was a trade-off I was willing to make, time with him for the time in the attic.

After Mom and Matt left, I saw Cooper out on the dock. We had not been allowed on either the pier or the dock until today. Uncle Joe had to make sure it was safe since it had been underwater during the surge of the storm. A few boards had to be nailed, but it made it through the storm surge without much damage. Uncle Joe said it was because it had been built with hurricane specs, whatever that is, and because it was new.

I quickly ran out to meet Cooper. He had a crab basket in the water and was catching a lot of crabs. The adults didn't have time to "mess with them," so he was just throwing them back. We laughed and jumped and screamed when one fell onto the dock. It would eventually find its way to the edge and jump back into the creek. The sun was hot, but there was a nice breeze blowing, and that meant no bugs. We crabbed and played until Aunt Sissy served us sandwiches and Coke.

After lunch, Aunt Sissy suggested that Cooper and I check with the neighbors to see if we could help. By now, most of the driveways had been cleaned, and the adults had picked up the debris from their yards. Everybody in the neighborhood would have to wait their turn to have the big trees cut and removed. Thankfully, there had only been minor damage to a few houses, but some of the wooded lots were devastated.

Most people who live on the coast have generators for such a time as this. Most of them had been through storms like this one. So there wasn't much to do except wander around jumping over trees. Cooper and I talked about the animals. Where are all the dead ones? Where did they go during the storm? Their treehouses had been twirled around and torn down, yet there were no dead animals, not even any injured ones.

I was actually enjoying being with Cooper, yet he was interfering with an opportunity to ask Aunt Sissy about the chest and its items. It was getting late in the afternoon, and I didn't know how to get him to go home. So I told him I needed to get cleaned up so that I could help Aunt Sissy cook dinner. He said that he was tired too.

As he turned to go down his drive, I blurted out the dumbest question, "Why hasn't your daddy checked on you all day?"

I wished I could have taken that stupid question back. It had been a good day. I had actually had fun with him exploring the neighborhood with its two lakes, walking trails, and wild animals. I tried to apologize, but there was no use. After a long glaring look, he turned and raced up the drive out of sight.

Chapter 6

I walked into a dark house. No one seemed to be home, but I knew Aunt Sissy would not leave me alone. I found her in a room on the bottom floor that was typically off-limits to everybody. It was her private place where she went for some quiet time. It was her place to get away from the madness of her world. The door was cracked, so I asked if I might go in. Surprisingly, she met me at the door and said, "I want to share something with you."

I was blown away; the room was filled with artwork, large paintings, and small ones. There were drawings in different stages of completion. I thought I was in an art gallery, the kind you read about in Italy where the famous artist just throws paint on a canvas, and they have a masterpiece. How did I not know about this room or my aunt's art?

"Your mom says that you draw all the time. She says that you should have been my daughter because the two of us are so much alike. She doesn't know how she was so blessed to have you with all of your talents."

I could not speak. My aunt was telling me things I had never heard or had the wildest idea that Mom felt that way. I always thought that I was in Mom's way. We had nothing in common. Where had I heard that before? Quickly, I recalled Aunt Sissy telling me that Mom and Grandmother had nothing in common. Not only was the attic in this house trying to steal my thoughts, but now this room and Aunt Sissy had joined with that force. It was almost more than I could comprehend.

The conversation quickly focused on her. She did the artwork when she needed self-gratification. She had gone through life not having adults understand her either. She said that she had always been compared to her mother, a free spirit. Her mother's life had not been pleasant. She had grown up during a time when kids had to work at an early age. Aunt Sissy's grandmother had died when Aunt Sissy's mother was young, and she had to help raise her siblings; no time to be free there.

I was barely audible when I finally asked, "Does Mom know about all of this?"

"Not really. She just thinks this is my workroom. She thinks I have job-related materials stored in here."

Then she told me this could be our secret. She said that I could draw or paint anytime I wanted as long as I closed the door. I had been given a secret passage to an unknown world, and I had been handed the key. Trembling, I raced over and hugged her. No words needed to be spoken. I had found another piece of me. I knew in that instant Aunt Sissy and I were joined at the heart. We had the same kindred spirit. Yet again, I knew this had changed a piece of me.

As we sat and ate dinner in the dimly lit room, I could think of very little except the art room. I needed time to explore. I wanted to see all the paintings and drawings. Had she ever shown any of them to anybody? There had been no conversation about anything in the room. She had told me about our kinship and how that kinship was shared with my grandmother. I wanted to know if she was troubled when she was in middle school. I wanted to know so many things.

I helped with the dishes and went to my room. On the bed lay a sketchbook with some pencils. The note simply read,

Show the world your heart.

My head was spinning. I could not think fast enough.

I had a wonderful day with Cooper, and yet I had offended him. I was truly sorry, but how could I tell him without having to be with him all day tomorrow? I thought of the ducks on the lake and how much I wanted to draw them. After all, I was trying to draw them the day I met Cooper. I thought about the art room and all that was hidden within its walls. I thought mostly about how my tolerance and fondness for Aunt Sissy had grown into an all-consuming mindscape. That was all I had thought about. It dawned on me that I had not thought about the chest in the attic, nor the spirit hidden inside.

The next day, the power was turned back on to Aunt Sissy's house. Aunt Sissy and Uncle Joe had gotten the debris cleaned from their house and yards, and everything was back in order. They could not return to their jobs because their offices in town still had no power, and the city still had major roads that were not navigable. Almost everything remained closed. Uncle Joe was going to try to go to the school to see if he could assist with getting the school cleaned for students to be able to return within a couple of weeks. Aunt Sissy was working in her home office and did not have time to spend with me.

I was torn between asking to spend time in the attic or to spend time in the art room. The answer was made for me when Aunt Sissy asked if I would tidy the art room. She gave me a short list of things to do. I think she knew I needed to search that room for some answers.

I had not been in there long when I heard Cooper asking Aunt Sissy if I wanted to go paddleboat riding on the big lake. I did, but not now. I had just settled down to look through a stack of old drawings. Why did he always do that? He had a knack for knowing how to rub me the wrong way. I thought back to the way I had ended yesterday and felt that I owed him an opportunity to have some fun. I walked out of the art room and closed the door. The last thing I wanted was for him to ask what I was doing. I had been given the key to a secret, and I was not going to give it away on day one.

I was still clutching my drawing pad and pencil when I walked into the kitchen where Cooper was talking to Aunt Sissy. Too late; he had seen the pad and would now want to see what I had been drawing, but he didn't ask. Most middle school boys grab your pad and make fun of whatever is on the page, not understanding that an artist doesn't want to share an unfinished project. Many artists don't want people to make judgments on unfinished work. He didn't. She knew that he was either really not interested or that he respected the feelings of another artist toward their work.

Did Aunt Sissy not feel good about her work? How could that be? It looked like a messy art gallery in that room, but it did look like a gallery. I would have to give this more thought when I had the chance to go back to my aunt's private room. I also wanted to know why Cooper had not asked to see my pad, but I would not ask at this time. I didn't want him to even think I cared or was interested.

We decided to go fishing in the large lake. Uncle Joe had shown us how to dig for worms in Aunt Sissy's flowerbed. So with a little work, we would always have fish bait. We were sworn to secrecy against telling Aunt Sissy about it. As we walked toward the lake, we spotted white-tailed deer tracks in the soft dirt around the lake. We had filled our pockets with corn to feed the ducks. The deer were always looking for any missed kernels. Cooper and I had named the ducks after an old TV show the *Three Stooges*. Harry, Curley, and Moe eagerly ate the corn out of our hands. Their nibbles tickled as they grabbed the kernels of corn.

While we were occupied with the ducks, we heard a huge splash in the lake. Cooper yelled, "What was that?"

I wasn't sure, but it was big and brown, and fish were jumping all around where it landed. I had seen an otter in the saltwater creek behind Aunt Sissy's house and in the smaller lake, but I had never seen one in this lake. Since the ducks were not squawking, we decided to enjoy our fishing trip but to keep an eye on the monster on the other side. We spent an hour catching fish and throwing them back. I won the race to see who could catch the biggest fish.

We decided to walk the hiking trails that were intertwined among the houses and wooded lots. With the slightest breeze, we heard small limbs fall as a result of the storm, so we had to be careful and look out for each other. One of the trails ran along the bank of a little stream. The stream looked like a creek with all of the extra water still draining out of the lakes. I loved this little stream. It had two waterfalls that rambled over old fallen wood logs. We talked about the possibility that a previous storm, from many years ago, might have created the waterfalls. The sound the falling water made was so soothing it would lull you to sleep. We heard birds singing in the distance. We wondered if they were singing happy songs because their homes had been spared or if they were trying to call to reach their families.

We walked and talked about everything we encountered, including that gigantic wood spider that hit Cooper right in the face. We both screamed. He screamed for my help, and I screamed because I was too scared to help him. We both brushed our arms vigorously over our heads and checked each other for the spider; screams turned to laughter. We never saw him on us, but we were covered in his web. After the running and laughter stopped, we talked about how we could win *America's Funniest Home Video* if someone had seen us.

We suddenly realized that we were hungry and raced to Aunt Sissy's to tell her that we were going to Cooper's house. He was going to make us peanut butter and jelly sandwiches for a picnic. Cooper's dad added cheese crackers and Cokes to our picnic bags. We raced back to the swing in Aunt Sissy's yard to enjoy our feast.

After lunch, we asked Cooper's dad and Aunt Sissy if we could use the two-seat paddleboat and play on the large lake. We wanted to check out the brown monster we had seen earlier that morning. With a life vest in hand, we headed back to the lake. We had been paddling around and playing with the ducks for about an hour when we realized that the grumpy old neighbor who lived on that lake was watching us. We started making up his life story. We wondered if he was grumpy because he lived alone, or did he live alone because he was grumpy.

I was amazed that Cooper played the same game I did when I met strangers. It was fun connecting people to their personal belongings and trying to tell their story. We quickly moved from that neighbor's story and started talking about other neighbors, wondering where they had been and how they had ended up in this neighborhood. We talked about everybody but ourselves. We would not cross the line of letting down our private walls, both scared of being hurt. I did have so many questions I wanted to ask him about his mother and his art. Once again, I enjoyed the day and didn't want to spoil it.

We spotted wild grapes hanging from a tree on the bank of the lake. They were out of reach. Then Cooper told me to stand on his back so that I could reach them. We spent the rest of the afternoon walking through the wooded lots, picking and eating wild grapes. We started talking about being contestants on *Survivor* and how we could make it to the end if we were on the same team. Then we realized we had not missed TV during all the chaos of the storm.

As we continued rambling the neighborhood, we passed a house with a pool. We talked about how that woman played in the pool every day. We joked about sneaking into her pool just for the fun of it since swimming in the lakes was not allowed without parents. Posted signs warned of snakes and alligators. We had seen alligators in the saltwater creek but not in the lakes. We thought the posted warning signs were just there to keep visitors from swimming. We had spent the whole day together, but I had not learned anything new about him. I had also not thought of the chest in the attic, nor the secret art room.

The next day, I was on the dock with my sketchpad when Cooper approached. He quickly sat down by me and took out his pad and pencil.

"What are you sketching this morning?"

While surprised, my words slid out like cheese from a tube.

"I saw the dolphins swimming in, so I'm waiting on them to swim out. I'm going to take a picture with my phone, and then I am going to draw them."

We both sat patiently and quietly, not wanting to ruin a chance to see the dolphins. The dolphins did not disappoint us. Soon a mother and her calf came swimming our way. It was so exciting to see them exhale, blowing the water out of their blowhole. We sat still, waiting for the opportunity to take a picture at the perfect time.

As soon as the dolphins swam out of sight, Cooper and I sat there in silence and began drawing the mother and her calf. We drew the concentric rings in the water they had made as they swam past. We tried to capture the glistening water on their backs as they had come up for air, but neither of us had quite mastered that technique. I dared if this was the time to tell Cooper that Aunt Sissy could teach them how to draw or if that would be breaking the secret bond I had made with her.

●

At that moment, Aunt Sissy came carrying glasses of lemon-ade. It was as though she knew I needed her. With a quick glance at our color pencil sketches, she sat between us and guided our hands and strokes. It was amazing. Cooper and I both produced beautiful sketches of the mother and calf dolphins. The blue water and green marsh grass framed our pictures. I don't understand why I wanted to share Aunt Sissy with Cooper, but at that time, I did. Thanks to Aunt Sissy, I didn't have to break our special bond. I knew that this would be another defining moment of this summer.

Chapter 7

For the next two or three days, we kept hearing that our schools had pushed their start dates back for a couple of weeks. Cooper and I were both okay with that; neither one looked forward to another year in middle school. We continued drawing animals that we saw in the neighborhood. We would take pictures of them and go back to Aunt Sissy's lanai to draw them. Aunt Sissy would come out and guide our sketches.

One day as we sat drawing an alligator that we had just seen in the creek, Aunt Sissy walked in with a shopping bag from the art store. She had bought both of us watercolor kits, not the cheap kid's kind but real authentic watercolor kits.

"If you are going to be an artist, you need to learn the right way."

We were in disbelief. She set up an area on her lanai and said that we could call it our art studio. We could not be torn away. Those colored pencil alligators were soon swimming in a creek of watercolor.

With her guidance, we were unstoppable. Neither of us asked her questions about how she knew how to teach art. I figured Cooper just thought it was because she was a teacher. I was scared that he would discover the secret room. That was my special bond with Aunt Sissy, and I didn't want it to include Cooper. He was not part of our spirit, and I didn't want him to ruin it.

I actually slept late the next morning. I was surprised that Cooper was not out on the dock with the crab baskets, and Aunt Sissy said she had not seen him. I decided since it was early in the day and the attic would not yet have heated up and because she and Uncle Joe were working that this would be the perfect time to ask to visit the attic. I approached the topic like a girl asking permission to go on her first date. I was giddy and yet frightfully optimistic.

I was struggling with how to approach Aunt Sissy when she just said, "Since Cooper is not here today, I thought you might like to go into the attic for some relics of your grandmother's art."

It happened as though I had dreamt it up. I could not believe that she actually asked me and even gave me permission to plunder. I tore up to my room and pulled on an old pair of jeans and a T-shirt and flew back downstairs.

"Okay, watch yourself now. There may be some nails hanging out of the rafters, and it will get hot sooner than you think. Your mother would probably not approve of either idea, the attic or your grandmother's artwork."

I wanted to dig deeper into that conversation. Right now, I had been given another key to the past, and I was going to make the most of it. This time, I made sure I had my cell phone. I wanted to look at everything at once. I had already noticed on my previous trip that there were old furniture and items draped in tarps propped up against the furniture. Those must be paintings, but the war in my head to look in that chest was beating out of control. The first thing I wanted to do was to quickly take pictures of the photos in the album. I could then share those with Aunt Sissy and compare them to the people I had been drawing in my sketchbook.

Once again, as I turned the pages, I became absorbed in trying to identify the story the picture was screaming to tell. I just didn't have enough information to set those people free. Besides, my grandmother was beckoning me to move faster. As I peeled off the layers in the chest, I discovered a gold mine of bracelets and trinkets. Why did my grandmother keep the ones she did, or did she simply keep everything? Surely, upon her death, her daughters split her jewelry. Why did my mother have none of this?

What was the story behind the trinkets? I know that all trinkets have a story. Even I kept certain trinkets in my bedroom, and everyone I kept held a special memory or moment in time. They all go together to tell the story of my life. My daddy always brings me bracelets from his journeys. Where had Grandmother gotten these bracelets? Were they from Granddaddy, or were they from a boy that she had liked while growing up?

At that moment, I thought back to Aunt Sissy's comment that Cooper wasn't home today. I wondered where he was. I also wanted to know how she knew that he wasn't home. Even more, why was I thinking about him while looking through this chest, a treasure trove of my grandmother's life? These were all questions I would think about later and possibly discuss with Aunt Sissy.

I was about halfway through the chest when Aunt Sissy called for me to come down, saying something about I needed to talk to Mom on her phone. Due to the heat, I knew I would not be allowed to return to the attic. So I quickly placed the items back in the chest in order.

As I was getting ready to leave the attic, I had to uncover at least one drawing. I quickly removed the tarp, and underneath the covering was my mom staring back at me. I was so startled I tripped over a box of rectangular shapes. What was that? I took two quick pictures of the painting and the box, covered the painting, and climbed out of the attic. I now had more questions than answers. I knew I would have to find a way to get back into the attic.

As I entered the kitchen, I saw Aunty Sissy talking with Mom. The news had just been announced that school would be starting face-to-face within the next week. Mom reminded me that we needed to go shopping for school clothes, so it was time for me to come home. For once in my life, I was not excited about shopping. I really wanted a few more days with Aunt Sissy. When I blurted out that I wanted to stay with Aunt Sissy for a few more days, I knew I had opened myself up for her next remark.

"Now, Abreea Louise, have you turned sweet on Cooper?"

My face turned red. I was suddenly furious, but I also knew that I could not tell her the truth. The truth was I had gotten closer to Aunt Sissy. We had so much in common, and I still had a thousand things I wanted to ask her. I also had to make at least one more trip to the attic. I wanted to find those letters. I didn't understand what was driving that feeling, but I just knew that my grandmother was trying to tell me something. I had to listen to the voice of that spirit that lived in the attic. So I just said nothing and endured what Mom thought was cute and funny.

Aunt Sissy came to my rescue.

"Sure, she can stay with me. I will take her home next Tuesday. What if she and I shop for school clothes here? Since it's a smaller town, there may not be as many people in the stores. I'll make sure she wears her mask and washes her hands. Besides, our schools have postponed their opening until after Labor Day. So kids here will have three more weeks to shop."

While I was happy for the chance to stay five more days, there was something in Aunt Sissy's conversation that bothered me, but I would think about that later.

After Mom's phone call, Aunt Sissy started making sandwiches for the two of us for lunch. I took the opportunity to ask her about things in the attic. I showed her the pictures of the box of items that looked like huge tapes and asked her what they were. She giggled and told me that those were VHS tapes, and that she and my mom used to watch them all the time. When I asked her why we don't use them anymore, she just laughed. She told me that those went "the way of the dinosaur." Discs replaced those tapes, and discs were replaced with cable TV that was replaced by TV on demand. I asked how I could play them, and she told me about a metal black box that should have been with the cardboard box of tapes. All I had to do was connect it to the TV.

After minutes of pleading, she agreed to connect it to the TV, and I could watch some of the movies if I would like to. I went back into the attic to get the tapes and the VHS tape player. She thought it would be a good afternoon activity for me to do during the heat of the day. She said that she would pop some popcorn, and I could invite Cooper over if I would like to do so.

Shortly after lunch, Cooper knocked on the deck door. I quickly ushered him inside with the excitement of the VHS tapes. He was as excited as I was. He had never seen anything like that either. We watched *Casper, Babe,* and were on the first *Free Willy* when Uncle Joe came into the room.

"You kids know that you can find every one of those movies on your TVs, don't you?"

Well, we did know that because Aunt Sissy had already filled us in on the history, but there was something magical about watching the same tapes that my mom and Aunt Sissy had watched when they were our ages. Besides, we had been having a movie afternoon with popcorn and Coke just like at the movies.

We had gotten so involved with the VHS tapes and the movies that I had not even asked Cooper where he had been all morning, nor did he offer to tell me. Soon, Cooper's dad called for him to go home to eat dinner, and that's how he left.

"Gotta go eat. See you later."

I decided that I would help Aunt Sissy cook dinner since I had nothing else to do. After dinner, I went to my room to look at the pictures I had taken with my phone. I couldn't wait for the perfect opportunity to discuss them with Aunt Sissy. I had five days, so I had to select the most important pictures to discuss first. I would plot a plan.

After a warm bath, I went to bed excited and happy. I had so much to think about. I was finally going back to school, and this was going to be my year. I was not going to be the same little timid, ugly duckling I had been last year. I was going shopping for school clothes with Aunt Sissy. I knew that my clothes would have a more colorful flare than if I had shopped with Mom. I had been to the attic. I had pictures from the photo album, and I had pictures of trinkets. I had seen a mysterious large painting that looked like my mother. I had a fun afternoon watching movies on VHS tapes with Cooper. Cooper! Where had he been this morning? Why had his daddy called him home so early? Why had he seemed extra nice, or were those just thoughts in my head because I had actually been to the movies with a boy! I had so many things to think about, and with that thought, I went to sleep.

Chapter 8

I woke up to the smell of my aunt's pancakes cooking. She made the best pancakes in all of Georgia and Florida. I ran downstairs to the aroma-filled kitchen and a warm hug from Aunt Sissy.

"I have a surprise for you today. I don't have to work, so I thought I would take you shopping. What do you say to us having a girl's day? Just the two of us?"

I was ecstatic! I was going to actually have a day with her by myself where I could ask her questions all day long. This was going to be a perfect day. We started our drive to Savannah by talking about what type of clothes I like to wear to school. She was actually asking me what I was interested in wearing, unlike my mom who would have taken me to one store and said, "Here, this would look good on you." My mother and I did not have the same taste in anything.

As we drove along the interstate, we began singing with the songs on the radio. Pushing a picture on my phone in her face, I asked, "Who is this? Tell me her story."

I don't know where it came from, but it came out of my mouth. I was just as surprised as Aunt Sissy.

"Is that from the album in the chest in the attic?" She took a deep sigh, and with that, the mood in the car changed. It was like the air had been sucked out through the vents. "You know, Abreea, we don't talk much about our mother, your grandmother. Your mom and I just don't remember the past the same way. We were two different kinds of kids, just like you and Matt. We liked different things and had different friends. I was more like your grandmother, but I didn't worry about things. I just didn't take everything to heart as your mother did, and still does.

"Your mother butted heads with your grandmother. They argued about everything. If I thought Mama was doing something to protect me or your mom, your mother understood it to be a bad thing. She believed that Mama was being mean to her. She constantly told me, 'Mama loves you more than me because you are just like her.'

"Your mom and I drifted apart when she went away to college and married your father. It wasn't until our mother died that she and I vowed to never let our personalities and our past separate us again. So by me telling you about your grandmother, I may be breaking the vow I made with her. I know that you are filled with questions. I know that you want more answers from the things up in the attic, but I can't break that vow with your mom."

So there it was! At least I had some answers. I now knew why she had allowed me to go into the attic and into her art room. I knew that she wanted me to discover my past to help me settle the issues I had with my mother. I knew that she did not want another generation of siblings to be apart because of differences related to my grandmother or because of broken relationships. I also knew that I was more like her than ever. We both knew that I would not stop searching until I had some of those answers. For now, I had to think about all she had said.

After what seemed to be forever, she quietly said, "That is your grandmother, and you are so much like her that your mother is scared she will lose you too."

I looked out the window so that Aunt Sissy could not see the tears rolling down my cheeks. She was right on several points. I would not stop the search. I now had a rumbling in my heart to know my grandmother. I also loved my mother. She got on my last nerve at times, but I loved her. I had to figure out a way I could set my grandmother's spirit inside of me free, without that spirit crushing my mom all over again.

We drove the rest of the way in silence, listening to the music playing softly in the background on the radio. When we started to walk away from the car, Aunt Sissy hugged me tighter than ever before.

"You will find your way!"

We spent a couple of hours shopping and trying on outlandish clothes, things I would never wear to school or even in public. While visiting one store, Aunt Sissy bought a little bracelet with a heart on it. By late noon, we decided to find a small local restaurant that Aunt Sissy said made the best homemade cinnamon rolls, and she was right!

While sharing our cinnamon rolls in the restaurant's garden, Aunt Sissy placed the bracelet on my wrist. One thing that I have always enjoyed is receiving little bracelets from my mom, dad, or Uncle Joe as souvenirs from their trips. I knew that this was a message about the trinkets in the attic. So this is how we would communicate. I loved the bracelet, but I loved her even more because she knew we shared that spirit from the attic. As we started to leave, Aunt Sissy purchased a few cinnamon rolls to take home for later. That was the first time today I had thought of Cooper. Maybe Cooper would like a hot cinnamon roll on the dock this afternoon.

As we drove home, we chatted loosely about the things we had seen in the stores. We talked about how some of the items looked like they were straight from the runways in Paris, and others looked like they were from antique closets. We talked about color, how for us it was as much about color as it was the design. Mostly, we talked about little nothings, just two conjoined hearts on a perfect journey.

Chapter 9

Just before getting home, I received a picture from Cooper on my phone. It was a picture of the Chattanooga, Tennessee, I-75 exit with the words

I bet you wish you were here!

I barely looked at the words. My mind was lost on the picture. What was he doing there and not at home? How long would he be gone? Who was he with? Had he known about the trip the day before when they were watching movies and had not told her?

Tears began to sting her eyes, but she could not let Aunt Sissy see her emotions. She didn't know which hurt worse, that he was not going to be back before she had to return home, or that he had left and not told her goodbye. He had not even mentioned it to her. Either way, she felt betrayed. She had let him into her inner space, and that had made her vulnerable. At the first chance, he had abused her trust.

She did not hear from him again until dinner when he sent a picture of himself with some other kid about his age eating in a restaurant in Kuttawa, Kentucky. Once again, the caption read

I bet you wish you were here!

The tears came faster and stung harder. This wasn't like the boy she had come to know, or was he exactly like that boy? Then she recounted their first meeting when he had been so obnoxious. It had taken her a long time to like him. Now she was sorry for that decision. By being his friend, she had allowed him to hurt her.

The next day was spent in Aunt Sissy's art room, just sitting and staring. She felt that was a safe place to get away from everyone and not have to talk about anything. After dinner, Uncle Joe invited her to go crabbing on the dock. She thought it would help to be in the fresh salty air.

Soon Cooper's dad walked over and began a conversation with Uncle Joe about an upcoming fishing trip and wanted to know if he was interested. About that time, I pulled in a huge crab. Cooper's dad was so excited when he remarked that Cooper surely had learned to enjoy crabbing. In fact, he had actually remarked how much he was beginning to like living in this community.

Uncle Joe, as though he could read my mind, asked, "Where is that young man?"

"Oh, one of Cooper's friends from Atlanta invited him to go on a trip to Montana since the school start date had been pushed back because of the pandemic. That friend's family has a cabin in Bozeman, Montana, on a river. Since it was to winterize it, his dad decided to take the boys and haul their dirt bikes so they could ride the trails around the lake. I drove Cooper to Atlanta early yesterday morning so they could leave Atlanta around noon. I think they spent the night somewhere in Kentucky."

The conversation continued, but I could no longer absorb what was being said. I didn't know whether to cry or scream. At least I knew the story and the game. Yeah, the game that he was now playing by sending pictures and the same hurtful remark with every picture. I would not play that game with him.

To cover my emotions, I continued to crab until it was dark. I didn't want to check my phone. I didn't want to know where he was spending the night, and I had to convince myself that I didn't care. He had betrayed our friendship, and I knew where I stood. After a few more pictures and even meaner remarks, the pictures and texts quit coming. She could no longer trust him as a friend. She had spent the summer searching for who she was, and now she felt like she was lost again, lost and all alone.

Now would be the perfect time to have a conversation with Aunt Sissy on making another trip into the attic to explore. I had seen the old painting in the attic and wanted to know about it. I had only gotten halfway through the chest and had not found the letters. Things were just not the same. The excitement had been sucked out of the air. The spirit in the attic no longer called to me. Had my grandmother turned her back to me just like she did to my mother? Is that why Mom struggled to find peace when she and Aunt Sissy tried to talk about my grandmother?

Nothing here was fun anymore. I could not talk with Aunt Sissy because of the promise she had made with my mother. I lost interest in the art room. What fun was exploring if you can't share it with someone or ask questions about your discoveries? Roaming the neighborhood was no longer fun. The hot days of August were unbearable. I looked forward to going home on Tuesday. If I was going to be miserable here, I could just as well be miserable in my own bedroom.

Chapter 10

Tuesday morning finally came, and Mom drove up to get me. After chatting endlessly with Aunt Sissy, she packed my things in the car, and we were on our way home. What had been a magical summer ended like all the rest.

Now I would go back to school and try to be that different person I had worked on all summer. This was the year I was going to be somebody. I was going to be popular. I had grown taller and gotten thinner. My short bob haircut had grown to chin length, and I was wearing it in different ways. I also had the new clothes that Aunt Sissy had helped me buy. If there was a high point, at least I liked my new style of clothes.

I was once told that you can put lipstick on a pig, but underneath you still have the same pig. I felt like that pig. I looked different on the outside, but on the inside, I still had the same insecurities I had always had. I was no closer to knowing who I was or who I wanted to be. I no longer felt a connection with the voice from the attic that had rattled me all summer. To top it off, I would have to wear a real mask to school. I would now have to struggle even harder to reveal the new person I had become over the summer. Now I just had another layer to hide behind.

School started just as it had in previous years with one major exception. It was a long boring day with everyone pulling on their masks and constantly taking them off their noses and faces. The teacher became a broken record, "Please wear your masks properly. None of us want to share germs. None of us want the virus."

I could not focus; there were just too many distractions. I was keenly aware that Cooper would be coming home on Saturday. At least I was not at my aunt's house. I would not have to hear his stories, nor would I have to tolerate his snide remarks. I needed to reconnect with my old friends and try to make new ones at school.

Friday afternoon could not come soon enough. I was a good student, but I didn't like not being able to chat with friends or go to music and art as we had in the past. The adults feared we would spread the virus if we got in close groups.

Upon getting home, I learned that Mom and Dad were waiting on us to get out of school. Two men who had chartered the fishing boat with Cooper's dad for the fishing trip had come down with the virus. They were looking for two people to take their places. My dad thought it would be a great trip for Matt and him. So Mom and I were going to spend the day with Aunt Sissy.

I was in disbelief. That was the last thing I wanted to do. How would I be able to dodge hanging around with the jerk since my mom and aunt thought that we had had a good summer together? How was I going to get out of this? Things were truly back to normal. Everything was about Matt! Not one person had asked me how I wanted to spend my first free day after being back in school, not one person!

The usual smell of pancakes hit my nose. At least that was one good thing about having to go to Aunt Sissy's. I knew it would go downhill after that.

It wasn't long before the conversation turned to Cooper's trip. Aunt Sissy was sharing with Mom and me all the great, fun things he had done while he was in Montana. He had been swimming in the cold river water. He had canoed down the river and spent the night camping out with some other guys and their dads. She talked about the things he had seen and the places he had been. She shared that he had eaten bison burgers. She was genuinely excited for him. He had had it so bad since his mother left, and being forced to move down here made it worse. It was time for him to get a break.

I sat there and endured the punishment. At one time, I might have been excited for him as well, but that was then. Eventually, Mom asked, "Is he back yet? I'm sure Abreea would love to get caught up on his trip."

I thought I was going to explode with instant anger. At that moment, I knew why my mom and my grandmother did not get along. I so resented that statement, and that smile on her face made me want to vomit. She was my mother, and yet she did not even know who I was. She doesn't know what I like or dislike. She doesn't know what I like to wear, places I like to go, or even what I like to eat. I needed to go to the attic! I had to find that spirit that had called me so strongly during the summer. I was so consumed by my thoughts that I almost missed the answer. He would not return until about the time for us to leave. I had been rescued.

We had been out on the dock feeling the change in the air when I saw lights pulling into his driveway. At about the same time, Dad announced that it had been a long day, and it was time for us to go. Saved again.

As we drove by his house, I could see him waving. This time I did not wave back. I had made that mistake one time, and I would not make it again. I had opened my heart for his friendship, and he abused it.

Yet I so desperately wanted to talk with him about the trip. I wanted to share with him what I had been doing for two weeks. I wanted to tell him the secrets the attic had revealed and about the time I had spent with Aunt Sissy and my grandmother. I wanted him to know the secrets the art room had exposed. These had been my safe places. Now they would have no meaning for him. They belonged to me, and I would keep it that way.

As we continued on our way home, I sank deeper into my thoughts from the summer. Suddenly, I shivered with a chill. I felt the spirit from the attic around me. I realized that I was stronger. I knew there would be more days ahead of facing the girl from the summer. The chest in the attic still held a myriad of unanswered questions. For now, I would be content knowing that Grandmother's spirit was no longer locked in that chest in the attic.

About the Author

Betty Ellis has been sharing her love of storytelling most of her adult life. For sixteen years she taught reading to fifth- and seventh-grade students. She is the mother of two grown children. She lives in Southeast Georgia with her husband and dog, Jack.